Famous
Illustrated Tales of
TENALI RAMAN

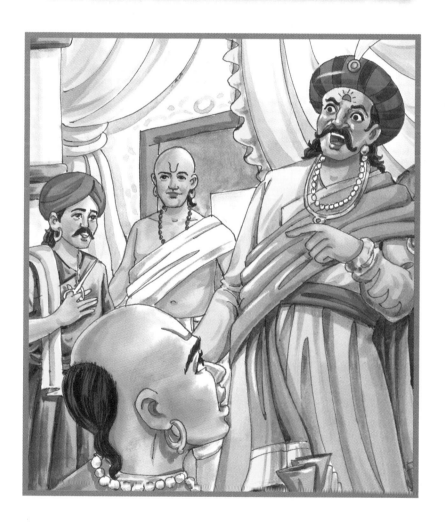

MAPLE KIDS

Famous Illustrated Tales of
TENALI RAMAN

Published by

MAPLE PRESS PRIVATE LIMITED

Corporate & Editorial Office
A 63, Sector 58, Noida 201 301, U.P., India

phone: +91 120 455 3581, 455 3583
email: info@maplepress.co.in
website: www.maplepress.co.in

Reprint in 2021

ISBN: 978-93-50338-45-2

Printed at: Rashtriya Printers, Delhi, India

10 9 8 7 6 5 4

Contents

1. An Advisor Who Told the Truth   4
2. The Golden Mangoes   8
3. Tenali Hides His Face   12
4. Barber's Reward   15
5. Tenali and the Thieves   19
6. Tenali Raman Decides to Paint   23
7. The Red Peacock   26
8. The Shrewd Businessman   30
9. The Palace of Dreams   34
10. The Weird Wedding Invitation   39
11. Who is Honest?   43
12. The Biggest Fool   47
13. The Scholar from Kashi   51
14. The Key to Heaven   57
15. Tenali and Sultan Adil Shah   59
16. The Invisible Cloth   64
17. Reciting of the Ramayana   69

An Advisor Who Told The Truth

Once upon a time, a brave and mighty king Krishnadevaraya ruled the vast empire of Vijayanagar. His capital was Hampi. However, Krishnadevaraya's court was called Bhuvana Vijayam. There were the *Ashta Diggajas*, the eight extraordinary men in Bhuvana Vijayam who were well-known for their exceptional qualities.

The *Ashta Diggajas* were Allasani Peddana, Nandi Thimmana, Dhurjati, Madayya Gari Mallana, Pingali Surana, Tenali Raman Krishnudu, Ayyala Raju Rama Bhadrudu and Rama Raja Bhushanudu. These men were outstanding scholars and very talented in their respective fields. They lived in the king's court and often helped him to make the right decisions. But, of all of them, the king favoured Tenali Raman because of his natural wit and sarcasm. He was the most skilled of the *Ashta Diggajas*.

One day, King Krishnadevaraya with his *Ashta Diggajas* went to inspect a newly built reservoir. Looking at the water, the king asked his scholars, "How does the water in this reservoir look like?"

Nandi Thimmana replied, "The water in this reservoir appears to be pure!" Madayya Gari Mallana said, "It is crystal clear and dazzling!"

In the same way, each scholar commented on the water as creatively as it was possible.

When it was Tenali Raman's turn, he said, "Your Highness, the water has taken the shape of the reservoir you have built."

Tenali Raman did not flatter the king and gave a simple answer. And this was precisely what the king desired— an advisor who told the truth. The king was happy, and he praised him for his honesty.

The Golden Mangoes

King Krishnadevaraya's mother was a pious woman. During her lifetime, she had visited many pilgrimage sites and performed many holy ceremonies. The king was devoted to his mother.

When she fell sick, the king ordered the best doctors in the city to treat her. But alas! She was quite old. The medicines were ineffective, and she eventually passed away.

While sick in bed, the king's mother requested mangoes. But she had left him forever before the king could arrange for it. This saddened the king. He often lamented for not fulfilling his mother's last wish.

The priests who were invited to perform her last rites came to know of this incident. They decided to trick the king for some gold. They said, "Your majesty, your mother had wished to taste sweet mangoes in her final days. But the wish was left unfulfilled. Therefore, for the peace of her spirit, you must donate golden mangoes to some priests."

The king believed the priests and readily agreed. He ordered ten mangoes made of solid gold and presented them to the priests. The priests were relieved that their plan had worked. They performed the ceremony and returned home with the fortune.

However, the wise Tenali Raman could not understand the logic the priests had given to the king. How could the golden mangoes in the hands of these priests appease the dead woman's spirit? He knew the priests had only tricked the king into giving them the gold. So, he decided to teach them a lesson.

After few days, he invited the priests to his house. He said to them, "My mother died a while back. But I think her spirit is not at peace yet. In her last days, she had wanted me to hit herself with a red-hot iron rod. But I couldn't do it and she passed away with this last wish in her heart. Like you had suggested that the king should donate golden mangoes to you for the peace of his mother's spirit, it should hold true in my case too. I must hit you all with this red-hot iron rod for the sake of my mother."

And with this, he pointed out the red-hot iron rod that his servant was holding.

The priests began to tremble with fear. They all fell at Tenali Raman's feet, begging for mercy. Tenali Raman asked them to return the golden mangoes to the king and beg his mercy instead.

So the next day, the king got back the golden mangoes as the greedy priests got a taste of their own medicine.

Tenali Hides His Face

Once, Tenali Raman decided to visit the royal art gallery. The art gallery had exquisite paintings that the king himself had collected. As Tenali Raman was walking through the gallery, he noticed a scantily dressed nymph in one of the paintings. Tenali Raman did not like it. "Women should be respected, even if it is art," he reasoned. So with a brush and some paint, he set off to work on the painting.

One of the courtiers who also happened to be visiting the gallery saw what Tenali was doing. He went to the king at once and told him everything he had seen. The king was furious. He ordered his guards to present Tenali before him. When Tenali approached the king, the king shouted angrily at him, "How dare you destroy my collection? Do not show your face in this court again." Tenali bowed in respect and left the court.

The next day he walked into the court, covering his head and face with a large earthen pot. Everyone in the court were puzzled. The king, who could not recognise Tenali, asked him who he was and why he was wearing a pot on his head.

Tenali bowed and replied, "Your majesty, I am Tenali Raman. Yesterday you had ordered me not to show my face in this court again. That's why I have hidden it with a pot."

The court burst out into laughter. Even the king could not stop himself from smiling. He forgave Tenali Raman and asked him to remove the pot from his head.

Barber's Reward

One morning, King Krishnadevaraya was resting in an armchair in his room.

When it was time for the king to shave, the barber of the royal palace entered the room and found the king still asleep. The barber began to wonder, "Should I leave and come back later? In that case, the king might punish me for being late.

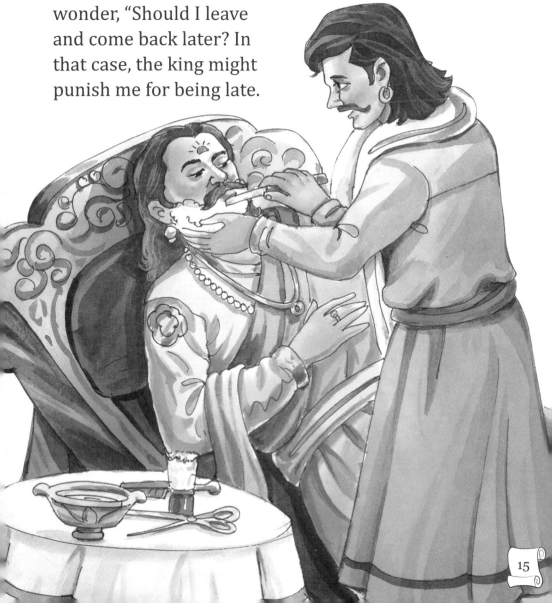

Should I wake him up? The king might then punish me for disturbing him. What do I do?" After much deliberation, the befuddled barber decided to shave the king's beard without waking him. He then left praying to the Almighty.

When the king got up after sometime, he decided to get a shave, so he called the barber. But, when he looked in the mirror, he was surprised to see that his beard had already been shaved.

The barber was scared that the king would punish him. When he came, he trembled with fright. On the other hand, the king said, "Dear fellow, I am very pleased with your skill and dedication towards your work. Tell me, what do you want in return? I promise I will do everything in my power to grant it."

The barber with folded hands said, "Your majesty, people of our kingdom look down on us. I want to become a priest so that people will respect me."

The king called the priests who suggested a ceremony to convert the barber into a priest. Even though none of the priests was enthusiastic about what was happening, they did not say anything because they did not want to offend the king.

The ceremony was scheduled on an auspicious day, and the king ordered for the preparations to begin. When Tenali Raman heard of it, he thought, "The king should not indulge in such stupid acts. I must tell him this."

Tenali Raman then found a black dog and took it to the pool near the royal gardens. He dipped the dog in the pool, combed its coat, and then dipped the dog in the pool again.

At that time, the king was strolling in the garden so he noticed Tenali. The king laughed and asked, "Tenali, why are you torturing the poor dog? Look at its eyes. It looks like it will begin to cry any minute."

"Your majesty," said Tenali, "I am only trying to convert it into a royal hunting dog." The king laughed harder. "Are you crazy? How is it possible to turn a black dog into a hunting dog by bathing?"

"Your majesty, if a barber can be converted into a priest through a ceremony, a black dog too can change by bathing. Can't it?" said Tenali.

The king had finally stopped laughing. He realised that Tenali was trying to tell him that a person has to be trained to gain skills. He cancelled the ceremony, and gave the barber a bag of gold and sent him home.

Tenali and The Thieves

One night, a few thieves decided to rob Tenali Raman's house. They crept into Tenali's backyard and hid behind a large drum, waiting for the

scholar and his wife to go to bed. Clever Tenali found out about the plan. But he knew that he was alone and not very strong enough to fight the thieves off. So he thought of a plan.

Tenali Raman collected all the gold and valuables in his house and stored them in a safe place. Then, in a loud voice, he told his wife, "Dear, I think we should hide all our gold and valuables in the well in our garden. Thieves have become very active these days. We never know when they might target our house."

Tenali then filled a large wooden box with bricks and stones. He took it to the well in his garden and dropped it.

With a loud splash, the box fell into the water and drowned. Tenali and his wife then put out the lights and went to bed.

The thieves in Tenali's backyard heard everything he said and the loud splash from the garden. They thought, "Why risk going into the house when the gold lies in the well?" So they went to check the well.

The thieves thought, "This little well is quite deep. We will drown if we try to go down into it to fetch the box." One of the thieves suggested, "Let's take the water out instead. When all the water in the well has been drawn, we will get the box easily."

The plan seemed good so they got down to work.

The thieves kept on drawing water from the well all night. All the plants in the garden were watered nicely when the sky turned purple with the dawn. But much to the thieves' disappointment, the well's water level did not drop by an inch.

Tenali Raman got up to find the thieves hard at work in his garden. He called out to them, "You may stop that now. All the plants have been watered."

The thieves were ashamed of their greed. They stopped drawing water and fled before the king's guards could catch them.

Tenali Raman Decides to Paint

Once, King Krishnadevaraya built a large mansion. He wished that its walls be decorated with paintings. A well-known painter was asked to take on the task. After a year, he reported that his work was complete. The king went to inspect the mansion with his *Ashta Diggajas* and several other courtiers. The work was truly exquisite and one-of-a-kind. The king was very impressed by the painter. He was proud of himself to get such an accomplished painter to do the job.

Just then, Tenali spotted that one of the figures did not have a limb. He pointed it out to the king. The king was taken by surprise. To get Tenali to overlook the defect, he said, "You must imagine the missing limb. That's the beauty of the painting."

Tenali was taken aback. He thought, "The king may have got a famous painter to do the paintings, but why would he not accept that there is a defect?" Tenali decided to make the king understand that one must always accept the truth, no matter how bitter it is.

After some days, he went to the king's court and said, "Your majesty, your mansion has inspired me to paint and today I have organised an exhibition of

my paintings. I would like to invite you to visit my exhibition." The king agreed.

When the king visited the exhibition, he was shocked to find that Tenali had hung strange paintings all around the room. On one canvas, there was a picture of a foot. On another canvas, there was a painting of a hand.

The king asked, "I am sorry, but I do not find these pictures very beautiful. You have only painted the limbs. Where is the rest of the person?"

Tenali smiled and said, "Your majesty, one must imagine the rest of the person. That is the beauty of these paintings."

The king was ashamed of himself. He realised what Tenali was referring to.

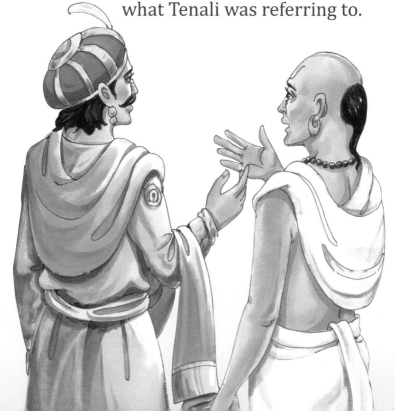

The Red Peacock

King Krishnadevaraya was very fond of birds. He had a vast collection of rare birds in his palace. One day, a courtier decided to get some favours from the king. He bought a peacock and hired a painter to paint it red. The painter did such a good job that the peacock looked as if it was naturally red.

The courtier then took the bird to the king and said, "Your majesty, this is the rarest kind of peacock in the world. It lives in a dense forest and is very difficult to catch. I have spent a huge amount of money to catch it for you. It will be a great addition to your collection."

The king was surprised as well as very pleased. He offered thousand gold coins to the courtier for the bird. The courtier was overjoyed that his trick had worked. He bowed to the king and left the court.

Tenali Raman who was present at the court suspected that something was not right with the peacock. When he went near the bird, he could smell the paint. He knew at once that the courtier had tricked the king.

The next day, Tenali bought five peacocks and asked his servant to find the painter who had painted the peacock for the courtier. The painter

was brought before Tenali, who then ordered the painter to paint the five birds. The painter painted the birds in red as he had done before. Tenali then took the birds and the painter to the court.

The king was shocked to see the five red peacocks, "The courtier said that this bird was the rarest of the rare. How did you manage to come across so many of them?" he asked Tenali.

Tenali first asked if the king would pay him a thousand gold coins for all five birds. The king agreed. Then Tenali said, "Your majesty, please come closer and sniff at the birds." When the king smelled the birds, he realised they were all painted. He was furious, "How dare you play a trick on me like that. I will sentence you to death!" Tenali said, "Your majesty, the bird that you had bought from your courtier the other day was also just another peacock painted red. This gentleman himself had done it." The king asked the painter, who confessed that the courtier had paid him to paint the peacock. Trembling, he said, "Your majesty, had I known that the courtier was planning to trick you, I would never have painted the peacock for him."

The king rewarded the painter for his excellent work, and the courtier was punished for his evil deed.

The Shrewd Businessman

King Krishnadevaraya often took pleasure in putting riddles across to Tenali Raman. One day the king asked, "Tenali tell me, people from which caste has the most intelligent people and which has the most stupid people?"

Tenali Raman thought for a while, "Your majesty, people from the businessmen community are the most intelligent and shrewd, while the priests are the most stupid."

On hearing this, the king was amazed. How could the most learned and wise priests be the most stupid of all people? He said, "Can you prove it?" Tenali said that he could.

Tenali then called upon the *rajguru*—the royal priest. He said, "Wise one, the king wishes that you have your *choti* off." The *choti* is a tuft of hair at the back of the head, which is left unshaven and represents a Hindu man's pride. The priest was taken aback. He said, "Your majesty, I have tended this *choti* for years now, and it is a symbol of my pride. But since you have desired, I would shave it off, but I would need something in return."

The king said he would grant any amount of money if the priest shaved his *choti*. So, the priest requested five gold coins. He took the money, shaved his *choti* in the court and left.

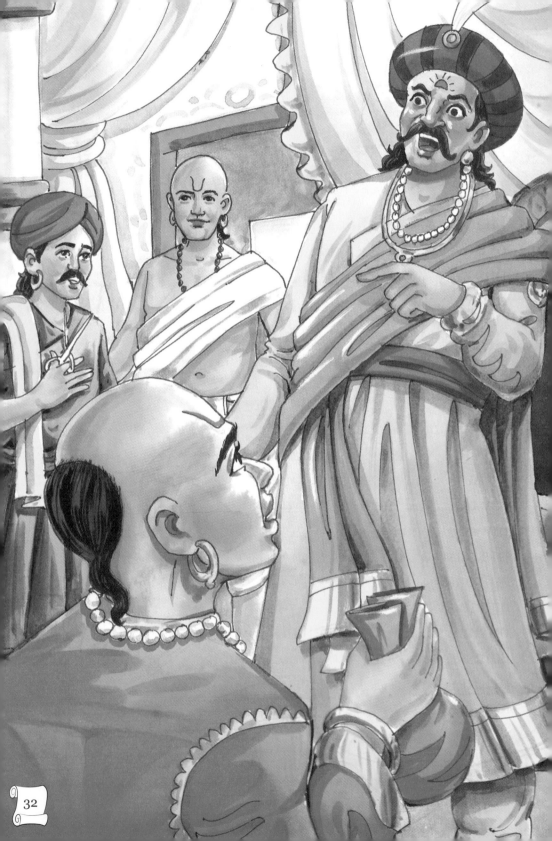

Tenali then called upon the richest businessman in the city. When the man learned of the king's wish, he said, "Your majesty, I will shave this *choti*, but I am a poor man. When my brother got married, I had to spend five thousand gold coins to keep this *choti*. Then when my daughter got married, I had to pay ten thousand gold coins for the sake of this *choti*. It has cost me a lot of money to keep this *choti*." The king said, "Your loss would be compensated if you have your *choti* off."

The businessman was given fifteen thousand gold coins, and when the barber proceeded to shave his *choti*, the businessman said, "Be careful. I have sold this *choti* to the king. It belongs to the king now. So be careful when you shave it. Don't forget that it is the king's *choti* that you are shaving."

At this, the king burst out angrily, "How dare you say that. You mean to say, that I am so crazy to have my *choti* shaved?" He ordered the guards to take the businessman away.

Tenali Raman smiled. When the king had calmed down, he said, "Do you realise how the businessman got to keep the fifteen thousand gold coins and his *choti* at the same time while the priest shaved his *choti* for just five gold coins?" The king praised Tenali for his exceptional judgement.

The Palace of Dreams

Once, King Krishnadevaraya was resting in one of the balconies of his palace. The moonbeams soothed him as he lay enjoying the breeze. Slowly he fell asleep, and soon he began to dream.

That night, the king dreamt of a magical palace that was floating in the air. Its white marble walls were decorated with colourful stones.

He grew feverish with the thought of owning a palace like that. He made a public declaration. "Whoever can build a palace like the one the king had dreamt would receive one lakh gold coins from the king." Soon after, the word spread and the streets of the city began warming with people from other cities. They all wanted to witness the miracle happen. The king's declaration became the talk of the town, and people wondered if the king had gone mad. How was such a palace even possible to build? Some greedy men even

conned the king for his money while they gave false hopes to him about building the palace of dreams.

A month passed. The ministers of the king's court were beginning to be uncomfortable. The king had stopped bothering about the affairs of the kingdom. Instead, he thought about the palace day and night. Finally, the ministers approached Tenali Raman.

Tenali had a plan. He went to the king and asked for a leave. Then after a few days, an old man came running into the king's court and fell at his feet. "Save me your majesty, my family will die of hunger!" he said. The shaggy old man stood sobbing in the court, "I have been robbed. I have been saving to get my daughter married, but the money is gone now. How will my daughter be married now? How will I feed my family? Everything is gone! Everything!"

The king was about to call the guards and ask them to find out who had robbed the poor fellow. But the old man said he knew who had robbed him, "It is you, your majesty, you have robbed me." The king was perplexed. "Me? You fool, I am the king. Why will I rob you? Besides, it has been a month I have been outside this palace," the king bellowed.

The old man said, "Last night I dreamt you came to my house with the royal guards and you took my money forcefully. I am a poor man, your majesty. You must consider that at least."

The king was boiling with anger. He said, "Are you crazy? Do you think dreams are real?" The old man said, "Why your majesty if the flying palace of your dreams can be real, why can't my dream be real?"

The king was shocked. Then he was ashamed. He thanked the old man for opening his eyes. The old man then removed his false beard and wig and bowed to the king. It was Tenali Raman himself. The court was applauding his intelligence.

The Weird Wedding Invitation

Once, Sultan Adil Shah, the ruler of Delhi during King Krishnadevaraya's reign, decided to wage war against Vijayanagar. However, the hostile sultan needed a reason to wage war. After all, one does not declare war on its allies just because one feels like it. So he began to look for a reason and soon came up with a plan.

The royal court of Vijayanagar was just beginning with its session that morning when a messenger from Delhi approached the king and produced before him, a wedding invitation. As the king read the invitation, his eyes grew wide with confusion and horror. Then the invitation was read aloud in the court. It said,

"We wish to perform the marriage of a newly dug well in our kingdom. We have the pleasure to invite all the wells of Vijayanagar to attend the ceremony."

Below the invitation, it said,

"In case you are unable

to send your wells, the ruler of Delhi shall be offended, and there will be consequences."

The king was in trouble. How was he supposed to send his wells to Delhi? The peace-loving king did not want war. So he sent for Tenali Raman.

When Tenali Raman read the invitation, he laughed. "The sultan sure has a good sense of humour. Do not worry, your majesty, I will write a good reply to this," he said.

The next day Tenali Raman came to the court with his reply. It said,

"To His Excellency, the sultan of Delhi,

It is kind of you to invite our wells for the wedding of a well in your empire. We are glad and grateful that you remembered us for the memorable occasion. On receiving your invitation, we immediately read the message to all the wells in our kingdom. They said that since your wells had not attended their wedding, they have a good mind to ignore this invitation.

Hence, we would like to suggest that if your wells personally come to Vijayanagar and invite our wells, our wells will definitely oblige the invitation. Therefore, it would be an honour if you kindly sent your wells here to invite our wells personally to the wedding ritual. Once your wells come here, our wells and we together will come to Delhi for the wedding.

We are hoping to welcome your wells at the earliest."

The king was relieved as he heard the reply. It was then sent with the messenger back to Delhi. The court burst into a "Bravo bravo!"

When the sultan received the reply, he understood that he had made a mistake. He decided to never try to trick King Krishnadevaraya again.

Who is Honest?

One day King Krishnadevaraya asked his court, "Who is more honest, a rich man or a poor man?" *Rajguru*, the royal priest, stood up and bowed. He said, "Your majesty, it is the rich man who is more

honest. He already has enough. So why will he wish for more and try to get it in dishonest ways?"

The king was not satisfied and wanted a different perspective. He asked Tenali Raman to answer. Tenali said, "I beg to differ, your majesty. I think it is the poor man who is always more honest than a rich man."

The king asked if he could prove it. Tenali said, "Of course, your majesty. But I will need some time and a bag of gold coins." The king agreed.

When Tenali was given the bag of gold coins, he divided the money equally in two purses. One purse he carefully placed on a road that a rich man often took. The rich man would pass by the road to the river for his daily bath. That day the bag fell to his notice. He got down from his carriage and picked it up. "Goddess Laxmi has blessed me. Today is my lucky day!" He thought as he pocketed the money and left.

Tenali Raman, who was hiding behind a tree, saw everything. The next day, he placed the other bag of gold in the path of a poor man. The poor man would often take this path to his fields. That day when he saw the bag, he picked it up and thought, "Some poor man must have lost his life's savings. I must do everything to return this to him. I have seen bad days because of poverty. I do not wish the same for this person."

He took the money to the royal treasury straight away and submitted it there. Tenali was again hiding behind a tree. He saw everything and was satisfied.

Tenali came back to the court and reported everything. The king was very pleased with the poor man and rewarded him. The rich man was punished for his dishonesty and had to pay a hefty fine.

As for Tenali Raman, his cleverness was praised by the king and his court once again.

The Biggest Fool

The king of Vijayanagara, Krishnadevaraya, was very fond of horses. One day, an Arabian horse trader approached the king and said, "Your Excellency, I have brought some horses from my country. Would you like to buy them?"

The king saw one sturdy horse that the trader owned. The king wanted to know what kind of horses the trader had. The trader said, "Your majesty, I have twenty horses to sell. They are of the best breed and as sturdy as this one. It was difficult to bring all the twenty horses to Vijayanagar so I have brought just one as a sample. If you like it, I can sell all the twenty horses to you for five thousand gold coins."

The king was overjoyed. He had indeed liked the horse. "What a wonderful sight would twenty such horses be! My stables will be best in the whole country," he thought. So he agreed to the proposal. However, the horse-trader said, "There is one thing, I would like you to pay in advance.

I promise to bring the twenty horses as soon as I get my payment." Though the king was unwilling, he paid the man the full amount in advance. The trader took the money and left.

Then months passed, and there was no sign of the Arabian trader. The king began to grow impatient. He kept pacing around his palace. One day when he was strolling in the gardens, he saw Tenali Raman feverishly scribbling something on a piece of paper.

"What are you writing?" the king asked. "Your majesty, I am making a list of fools in the city," Tenali said. "Show me," said the king. "I am sorry, your majesty, I cannot show it to you," replied Tenali. "Why?" the king asked. Tenali was silent. The king snatched the paper from his hands.

He was shocked as he read the list. "How dare you!" the king bellowed. "You dare show your king such impudence? How dare you put my name at the top of the list?"

Tenali was calm. "Because your majesty, any man who would give five thousand gold coins to a stranger and expect him to return is the biggest fool."

The king said, "How do you know for sure that he will not return? What if he does return?"

"Then, your majesty," said Tenali, "I would strike out your name from the list and write his."

The king did not question Tenali further. He handed the list back and walked away from the garden.

The Scholar from Kashi

Once in King Krishnadevaraya's court came a renowned scholar from Kashi. He had travelled many parts of India and was known to have been very well-versed in all subjects. The scholar enjoyed debating with other scholars and was proud that he had never been defeated.

When he came to Vijayanagar, King Krishnadevaraya welcomed him with respect and invited him to stay at the royal palace. The scholar agreed, and they stayed in the palace for a month. But then the scholar grew tired of his luxurious life at the palace and wanted to have some fun. So one day, he proposed to the king, "Your majesty, I have heard that you have great scholars in your court. I would like to challenge them to a debate. If they win, they will have all my titles but if I win, they will have to take me as their master."

The king was puzzled. He called the *Ashta Diggajas*. All seven of them arrived. They too were perplexed at the proposal. None of them volunteered as they were scared of the scholar's titles and testimonials.

The king called for Tenali Raman. Tenali was tending to his garden when he was told that the king had asked for him. He came running to the court. The king asked if Tenali would want to participate in the competition. Tenali agreed.

The next day, the scholar from Kashi arrived in the court dressed in fine silk and his medals, all set for the competition. But he stood wide-eyed as he noticed his competitor.

Seven scholars walked, singing praises of Tenali as Tenali walked behind them, wearing a silk dhoti and a shawl embroidered with fine gold. He also wore medals studded with precious stones. His forehead was smeared with vermilion and sacred ash. Servants placed bricks of gold before his feet, and under his arm, he carried a big book covered with the finest silk.

The scholar from Kashi was dumbfounded at sight. Tenali Raman sat at the desk and opened his book. Then he looked around and asked arrogantly, "Who is the scholar who wishes to debate with me?" The scholar from Kashi stood up. "I am the scholar," he said, trying his best not to sound shocked.

The king declared the debate to begin, and Tenali invited the scholar to a debate on the book he had brought. The scholar asked, "May I know what is that book you are carrying." "It is called *Tilakashtamahishabandhana,*" Tenali said.

The scholar had never heard of that book before. He thought, "I must avoid having the debate as

I have never heard of this book, and this man looks like someone who can easily defeat me." He respectfully bowed to the king and said, "Your majesty, I remember to have read this book a long time back. I request you to give me a day to brush

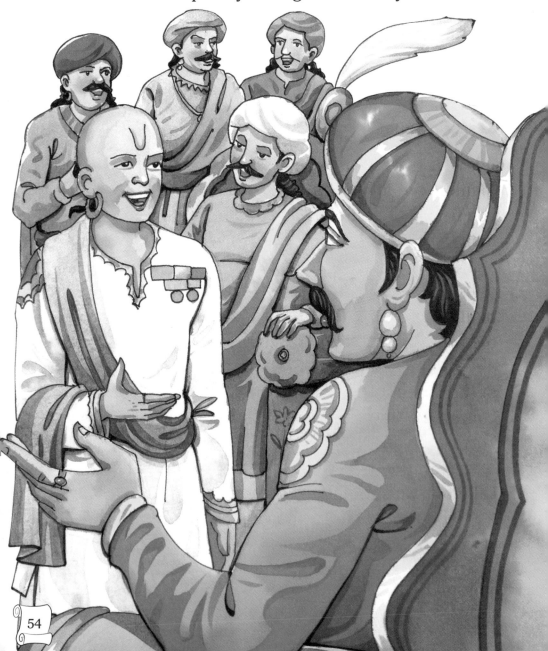

up my memory of this book before we proceed with the debate." The king agreed, and the scholar returned to his chambers.

He began to pack his things hastily, and that very night, he and his disciples quietly left the palace, and never returned back.

When the king heard about it the next morning, he laughed in surprise. He called for Tenali to give him the good news. When Tenali came to the court, the king asked, "What was the classic that scared the learned scholar so much?"

"Your majesty, this is no classic. This is just a blank notebook I wrapped in silk," Tenali said. "So you lied to the scholar? That does not suit a learned man like you," said the king.

"Your majesty, with due respect, I did not for once lie. Here look, this is a twig from a sesame plant, and I have tied a rope that we use for tying buffaloes around it," and saying this, Tenali drew a twig which had a rope around it from the folds of the notebook. The king was amazed. Tenali continued, "In Sanskrit, '*tila*' means sesame, '*kashta*' means a stick, a buffalo is a '*mahisha*', and '*bandhana*' is that which binds. Thus I said it was called *Tilakashtamahishabandhana*."

"That should teach the scholar a lesson," the king said while bursting into peals of laughter. Later he rewarded Tenali Raman for his cleverness.

The Key to Heaven

In Krishnadevaraya's kingdom once, there came a sage. The people were overjoyed as rumours said that the holy sage could perform miracles. People from far and near visited him and offered him food and donated money.

Tenali Raman was not satisfied. He sensed that something was wrong. So he decided to see for himself. He went to the place where many people had gathered for a ritual. The sage was sitting in the middle with his eyes closed. He was reciting something.

Tenali decided to read the sage's lips as to what chants he was reciting. Tenali Raman was a learned scholar. He soon understood that the sage was a fraud, and it was nothing but some mumbo jumbo that he was muttering. He decided to teach the sage a lesson.

Getting up from his seat, he walked to the sage and pulled out a hair from the sage's beard. "I have got the key to the heavens," he declared. "He is such a great man that if you keep a hair from his beard, you shall go straight to the heavens after you die." The sage was shocked and hurt from the yanking, realised what was about to happen. The people chased him as he sprang from his spot and ran for dear life.

Tenali and Sultan Adil Shah

During King Krishnadevaraya's reign in Vijayanagar, Sultan Adil Shah ruled Delhi. A war broke out between the two provinces. It continued for several days when the two kings realised that enough lives had been lost, and it was time that they signed a treaty of peace.

King Krishnadevaraya was thus invited by Sultan Adil Shah to Delhi to sign the treaty. The king, with his courtiers, travelled to the sultan's kingdom. He hoped to establish a good relationship with the sultan.

At Delhi, King Krishnadevaraya was given a red carpet welcome. Everything was carefully arranged for his comforts. His ministers and scholars were given royal guest rooms and were very well treated. This impressed the king, and he began to hold high regard for the sultan.

But one day as they were sitting across the dinner table, Sultan Adil Shah told the king that he was very interested in Hindu mythology. He called upon a scholar who then recited some scenes from the Mahabharata, the ancient story where two clans of cousins—The Pandavas and the Kauravas, fought for the kingdom of Hastinapur.

When the recitation was over, Adil Shah asked Krishnadevaraya for a favour. He said, "Great king, I have heard a lot about the scholars of your court. It would be an honour if you would have them re-write the Mahabharata with me and my friends as the Pandavas, and you and your friends as the Kauravas."

King Krishnadevaraya was in trouble. "How is that possible? Mahabharata is a sacred text. How will my scholars ever be able to re-write such a sacred text?" But he couldn't refuse the sultan. He promised to talk to the scholars of his court about this.

Later in the day, he called a meeting with his scholars. All of them seemed worried. It was indeed a problem which seemed to have no solution. Suddenly the king remembered Tenali Raman. He said, "Tenali Raman, you have solved many difficult problems before. Tell me, how do we get past this one?"

Tenali bowed to the king. He said, "Give me a day, and I will fix everything." Having no other option, the king decided to leave it to Tenali Raman.

The next day Tenali approached the sultan in his court. With folded hands, he said, "Your majesty, as you have requested, our team of scholars have begun rewriting the Mahabharata. But there seems to be one problem." The sultan asked Tenali to say

what it was, but Tenali refused, saying that it would be inappropriate to say it in the court. He must schedule a meeting with the sultan alone.

The sultan agreed. Thus, in the evening, the sultan sent for Tenali. Tenali bowed respectfully and said, "Your majesty, we are really honoured by the responsibility that you have given us. But there is a problem. The Pandavas in the Mahabharata were five brothers who were married to one woman, Draupadi. Since you have requested that we portray you as the noble elder brother and your friends as the other four brothers, we are unable to do so thinking about your prestige..."

Before Tenali could finish his sentence, the sultan stopped him. Flying into anger, he said, "This is inappropriate. Please ask your team to stop the work at once. I shall not have the Mahabharata rewritten."

"But huzoor...," Tenali tried to argue, but Adil Shah stopped him again, "Look poet, I will not accept this. Stop the work at once, if you want peace for your people. You stop writing, and I will see that Delhi remains an ally to Vijayanagar." And with this, Adil Shah stomped out of the room.

Tenali went to give his king the good news. All the scholars and the king praised Tenali for his cleverness.

The Invisible Cloth

One day, a very beautiful woman came to king Krishnadevaraya's court. She was so beautiful that all the people in the court were dumbfounded. They fell silent as she walked up to the king and bowed respectfully.

"Your majesty," she said. "I am a weaver, and my team has perfected the art of magical weaving. I have brought a sample for you." She opened a tiny matchbox and brought out a silk *saree* from inside it. The cloth was so soft and so light that the king was bewildered.

"This is like air!" he exclaimed. "Yes, your majesty. It is a special technique that we use to weave such exotic cloth. However, we are working on a new project these days. We are designing a cloth which is lighter, thinner and softer than this *saree*. We call it the celestial cloth because only the gods are known to have worn it so far."

The king and his court listened carefully as the woman's intoxicating voice echoed through the great hall. The king said, "All right, I will fund the project. But you will have to present a sample to me after your research is complete." The woman agreed, and with the large bag of gold coins that the king gave her, she left.

Days passed. Then months passed. The king

grew restless as there was still no sign of the woman. Finally, he sent some of his ministers and guards to the place where she said her workshop was. When they reached the workshop, they were astonished at what they saw.

There were looms, but there was no thread. Seven weavers worked on it and they were so absorbed in their work that none of them noticed the troop of men standing there looking at them in amazement.

The looms worked, but there was no cloth that came out of it. They returned to the court and reported this strange happening. The king was furious. He sent for the woman at once.

The woman arrived with a servant girl carrying an empty plate. They bowed to the king, and the woman said, "Your majesty, I have brought the sample you had asked for." And the servant girl proceeded to present the empty plate to the king.

The king opened his mouth to say that the plate was empty when the woman spoke again, "Your majesty, this is a sample of the celestial cloth. It is invisible to ordinary human beings. But those who are very intelligent and wise can see how splendid it is."

The men who had gone to visit the workshop were shocked to hear this. They began to think, "Did we give the king an impression that we were not

wise but fools? Then this is the time to set it right."
They approached the king and said, "Your majesty,
what a splendid material this is. The embroidery is
exquisite. It is a delightful thing and truly fits a king."

On hearing this, the king was confused. He was
in trouble. If he said he couldn't see any cloth, his
subjects would think he was a fool. If he said he
could see the cloth, the woman would con him of
his money and get away with it. The king gestured
Tenali Raman to come near him, and he whispered
everything into the wise man's ear.

Tenali Raman smiled. He turned to the woman
and said, "Lady, we appreciate your talent. It is
indeed a pleasure to accept this great piece of
celestial cloth. But with due respect, the king
requests you to kindly wear the cloth in the court so
that we may admire how beautiful it looks on
a person."

The woman understood that her trick
had backfired. She could either accept
her mistake or stand without clothes
in public. She fell at the king's feet and
begged for his mercy. The king was
kind, so he forgave the
woman. However, she
had to return the bag
of gold she had taken
from him.

Reciting of The Ramayana

When King Krishnadevaraya ruled the kingdom of Vijayanagar, a small city called Vikrama Simhapuri was much talked about. People often talked about its courtesans, who were exceptionally cunning and cruel. The most cunning amongst them was Kanchana Mala.

Kanchana Mala would challenge a scholar to a recital of the Ramayana. The task was to be able to satisfy her with the recital. If she says she

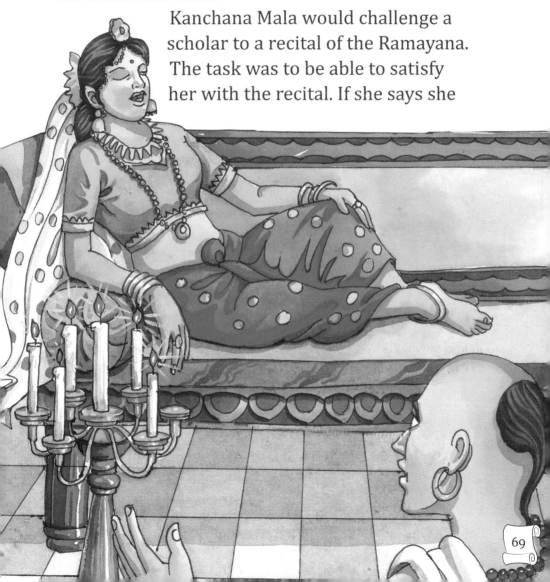

is satisfied, the scholar would win. If not, he would have to remain as a slave to her.

Kanchana Mala was so cunning that she never said she was satisfied, no matter how good the recital was. That way, she had enslaved many scholars.

One day Tenali Raman decided to beat this woman in her own game and free all the men. Upon reaching Kanchana Mala's house, he declared, "I have come to accept Kanchan Mala's challenge."

"Do you suppose you are aware of the conditions?" Kanchana Mala asked. Tenali Raman agreed, and the recitation began. The room they sat in smelled lovely because of the perfumed candles and was decorated with satin. Tenali began to recite the Ramayana. It was the story of King Dasharatha, who ruled Ayodha. He had four sons— Rama, Laxamana, Bharata and Shatrughana. Tenali Raman described how the king was forced to send his eldest son Rama into the forest and his wife Sita and younger brother Laxmana accompanied him.

Tenali then very beautifully described their life in the forest, and he dramatically told of how the evil king Ravana kidnapped Rama's wife Sita.

But it was all in vain as Kanchana Mala yawned loudly and lay down on the soft bed. It was clear that she was bored.

Tenali Raman then described how Rama and Laxmana, having lost Sita, walked in the forest in their grief and met a band of monkeys. How then Hanuman, one of the monkeys, offered his devotion to Rama, and carried his message to Sita in the evil king Ravana's city, Lanka.

Kanchana Mala rolled over and said, "I am not

satisfied. You are such a boring man. I wish there was more drama."

Suddenly, Tenali Raman leaped up from where he was sitting. He said, "This is how Hanuman leaped from one mountain to another!" and he leaped on the bed where Kanchana Mala was lying and from there, he leaped onto another bed nearby.

"This is how Hanuman crossed the vast sea," Tenali said and then leaped over Kanchana Mala. Kanchana Mala screamed in shock. Tenali said, "This is how Hanuman fought everyone who tried to capture him," and he began to punch Kanchana Mala's back with his fists. The poor woman was now howling with pain.

Then Tenali took the candle and said, "When they set Hanuman's tail on fire, this is how he set fire to the whole city." And Tenali set fire to the curtains and drapes. Within moments the room was on fire.

Poor Kanchana Mala was forced to flee her home for dear life. Tenali had set the whole house on fire. She was furious. The next day, she went to the court and complained against Tenali. When the king asked Tenali, he said, "Your majesty, this woman had been tricking scholars and enslaving them. I was left with no choice."

The king, on hearing this, gave his judgement in favour of Tenali Raman. Kachana Mala had to release all the men she had enslaved and pay a hefty fine for cheating.